THE LiZZIE McGUIRE MOVIE

Adapted by J. G. Weiss and Bobbi Weiss
Based on the screenplay written by
Susan Estelle Jansen and Ed Decter & John J. Strauss

Disney
PRESS

New York

D0052907

Printed in the United States of America

First Edition
3 5 7 9 10 8 6 4 2

Library of Congress Catalog Card Number on file.

ISBN 0-7868-4584-8
For more Disney Press fun, visit www.disneybooks.com
Visit LizzieMcGuire.com

CHAPTER 1

Today was a very big day for Lizzie McGuire. It was graduation day. Good-bye, Hillridge Junior High School! Hello, brand-new, unhumiliating life!

Lizzie was getting ready in her bedroom, singing along with the radio, blissfully unaware of the evil about to be unleashed upon her.

Only a room away, Matthew McGuire, little brother and official Lizzie Tormentor, was putting his latest plan into action. He'd already wedged his little digital video camera under the hood of his radio-controlled police car. Now he slipped a videotape labeled *Blackmail* into the tape player and hit RECORD.

"Some say, juvenile," he whispered to himself with an evil chuckle. "I say, genius!"

When Lizzie heard a thump on her bedroom door, she immediately stopped singing and opened it.

In zoomed a remote-control police car. "Matt!" she shouted angrily, slamming the door and trapping the car inside. This was *so* not the time for stupid pranks. "Say good-bye to your little toy!" she yelled.

Little did she know that she was doing exactly what Matt wanted. Her every embarrassing move was now being recorded, and Matt was watching her every embarrassing move on his computer screen. "And say hello to Matt owning his big sister for eternity," he said.

Thinking she was alone, Lizzie began singing into her hairbrush "microphone," applying makeup, and doing a little dance across the floor. Lizzie began rooting through her closet for a graduation outfit. She was looking for something special. Something that said, I am stylin', yet serious about my future. But there wasn't an article of clothing that said anything remotely close to that.

Quickly she painted her toenails, polished her fingernails, applied lip gloss, checked it out, then wiped it off. *So* not her color.

And then Lizzie began to sing again. As she lost herself in the music, her voice began to rise. Lizzie didn't usually sing loudly. It wasn't that she didn't have a good singing voice—quite the opposite. Lizzie had a great voice. She was just too shy to let anybody hear it.

Lizzie began to dance, twisting and twirling and singing away, right into her bathroom.

Disaster came swiftly—she tripped over the bath mat, and down she went, squealing and thumping and taking the shower curtain with her. She landed in the bathtub. Burning with humiliation, she just lay there, covered by the shower curtain.

Matt watched from his room with complete and total satisfaction. Slowly and seriously he rose to his feet. "I shall win the Academy Award," he pronounced.

CHAPTER 2

Lizzie, followed by Matt and Mr. and Mrs. McGuire, walked slowly and carefully into the auditorium. It took very precise movements to stay balanced on her stiltlike shoes.

Lizzie looked around the auditorium. Everyone was there—Lizzie's classmates, their parents, family, and friends, the entire faculty, the school staff. The last thing she wanted to do was trip in front of them all. She was determined not to do anything today that would result in public humiliation. Her mom looked at her with glistening eyes. "Honey, just yesterday you were in diapers—now you've graduated junior high, and you're growing up, going to Rome for two weeks all by yourself. Without me. Without me there. Without me with you. You there. Without me."

Lizzie rolled her eyes. "That's just about all the combinations of those words you can make, Mom."

Just then, her father placed his hands on her shoulders. "Lizzie," he said, his eyes full of love, "this is a big day."

He's going to quote a dead guy!

Mr. McGuire cleared his throat. "As

William Shakespeare once wrote, 'Be not afraid of greatness: some are born great, some achieve greatness, and some have greatness thrust upon them.'"

"Um, thanks, Dad, but I'm just trying to get through graduation," Lizzie replied. "'Greatness' can wait until this nightmare's over."

After her parents kissed her, Lizzie joined the huge group of graduates. Would she ever find her friends? Just then, she spotted Gordo. Good old Gordo. He was smart and funny, and he was Lizzie's best guy friend in the world. "Do I look okay?" she asked when she reached him.

"Lizzie, I'm your guy best friend. You should have talked about this with Miranda," Gordo said.

"But she's in Mexico City!" Lizzie protested.

Gordo sighed. "Yeah, your black robe looks

much hotter than all the other girls'," he replied sarcastically.

Lizzie nodded, then began running through the events of the day. "Okay, good. Fifteen paces to the principal. Take the diploma with my left hand, shake with my right hand. Smile and wave. Go back to my seat. And it's 'Later, junior high,' and we're on the class trip to Rome. Nothing can rattle me." She nodded to herself.

"Oh. My. God."

Lizzie whirled around to find Kate Sanders gawking at her.

"Only you would think that you could hide the powder blue, puffy-sleeved, it's-kind-of-a-peasant-dress-but-it-might-be-just-a-baggy-disaster-of-questionable-fiber-content that you wore to the spring dance!" Kate said. To prove her point, she unzipped Lizzie's robe, revealing said dress. At that very moment, the marching band stopped playing, and every member of the audience heard the following words: "Lizzie McGuire, you are an outfit repeater!"

Maybe I'm an outfit repeater, but you're an outfit rememberer, which is just as pathetic.

Lizzie had the awful feeling that her embarrassment was written all over her face, so it was a good thing she didn't know that Matt was capturing it on his video camera.

"Thanks for noticing," she muttered to Kate before Gordo dragged her away. "Doesn't she have anything better to do than make me feel bad?" she moaned. "We used to be best friends."

"Yeah, but, that was *before* she became popular," Gordo said. "You're a living reminder that she was once a geek, so she does every-thing in her power to destroy you."

Lizzie looked around her. "Well, that's all about to change," she said with determination. "By the end of today, we are *high school* stu-dents. I get to hit the RESET button on my life."

"McGuire!" barked a familiar voice.

Lizzie turned around to find Mr. Escobar, the school's drama teacher, towering over her. He smelled funny, sort of like the spicy cook-ies her grandmother made every Christmas. "Hey, Mr. Escobar. Nice aftershave," she said.

Mr. Escobar ignored the comment. "Margaret Chan either has Ebola or a really bad cold," he said sharply. "You're delivering the class president's speech."

WHAT?! Every nerve in Lizzie's body screamed in terror. "Wh-what about the vice president?" she stammered.

"He's not graduating," Mr. Escobar informed her flatly. "The secretary treasurer is next in line. I want you to deliver your speech with as much pride and commitment as Margaret Chan would have done, even though you're no Margaret Chan." He began herding her toward the podium as the band began to play again.

Okay, so it's fifteen steps. Give a speech to hundreds of people. Diploma with my left hand. Shake with my right hand. Smile and wave. Then it's our class trip to Rome!

"Ladies and gentlemen, Margaret Chan!" said a booming voice. "Check that, Mizzie McGuire!"

With all eyes on her, Lizzie walked very carefully to the podium and gazed out over the crowd. Everybody fell silent and stared back at her, waiting. And waiting.

Lizzie tapped the microphone, hoping maybe it was turned off. No such luck—one little tap, and a noise like all the fingernails in the world scratching a blackboard shrieked through the auditorium. Everybody jumped.

Lizzie gulped, hearing Kate's words echo through her mind: Oh. My. God.

"Margaret Chan couldn't be with us tonight, so I will be taking her place," Lizzie said, managing a smile. Did she just say that? Hey, good beginning! "Well, not that anyone could really do that," she found herself adding. Nobody laughed, so she plunged ahead. "I think we all agree that junior high was filled with embarrassing, awkward, and sometimes even downright humiliating moments. Right?" Complete silence. "Me, neither . . ."

Oh, why couldn't a bolt of lightning just strike her now and end the torment? But then Lizzie caught sight of Gordo. He mimed drinking a glass of water. Good idea!

"I think Margaret would want me to drink some water now," Lizzie said. She retreated to a table with glasses of water on it near the back of the stage. Good old Gordo! Maybe if she drank really slowly, a brilliant idea would come to her and she'd give the greatest speech in Hillridge Junior High history!

Nope. Instead of finding inspiration, Lizzie McGuire found humiliation. One of her platforms snagged a power cord. She started to fall, arms pinwheeling in a desperate search for something to grab onto. Fortunately, she found something. *Unfortunately*, it was the stage curtain. In a horrifying reenactment of her disastrous bathroom gig that morning, Lizzie hit the floor like a bag of sand, pulling the entire stage curtain down with her, covering herself, the faculty who were sitting on the stage, and the entire school band.

Things could *not* have gone any worse.

CHAPTER 3

The next morning, Lizzie burst through the doors of the airport terminal, anxious to find Gordo and her other classmates going on the Italian trip, board the plane, and get as far away from her old school as possible. After a few days in Rome, no one would remember the graduation disaster. Right?

"Mom, Dad, please, let's go," she said to her parents, who were dawdling, as usual. "I need to leave the country now."

"Sweetheart, please," said Mrs. McGuire. "We know you're upset, but it wasn't that bad."

"Oh, really, Mom?" said Lizzie. "Was your junior high graduation on *Good Morning America*?"

Mr. McGuire shook his head sadly. "What kind of creep would send Diane Sawyer a video and embarrass you like that?" he asked.

Matt, who was taping the entire conversation, hid his smile as the McGuires joined a group of Lizzie's fellow graduates and their parents who were gathering in the terminal.

Just then, the blare of a horn cut all conversation short, and the little crowd parted to make way for a golf cart driven by an airport employee and carrying one very preppy passenger. Her hair was meticulously coiffed and held in place by a dainty headband, and she was wearing a Fair Isle sweater and penny loafers. But when the cart came to a stop and the woman stepped out to join the group, it was clear to Lizzie that this woman was no shrinking violet.

Gordo spotted Lizzie and her family and came over. "That's Miss Ungermeyer," he explained. "She's going to be our high school principal for the next four years. If you're on her good side, it's a one-way ticket to an Ivy League school."

"What if you're on her bad side?" Matt asked.

A janitor with a mop and wringer pushed past them, heading for the men's room. "Excuse me, people!" he said. "I need to mop up some puke!"

Gordo pointed at him.

"You end up that guy?" Matt asked.

"You end up *working* for that guy," Gordo said.

Lizzie studied Miss Ungermeyer. Geez, what kind of woman was she, part principal, part pit bull? All the students who were going on the Rome class trip were gathering together while all their parents were gathering around Miss Ungermeyer. The woman radiated confidence and control as parents shouted at her.

"Can you make sure there's no garlic or soy products in anything my Brittany puts near her mouth?" asked one mother.

"Luke has tennis elbow," said a father. "Could someone carry his luggage?"

On and on the parents prattled until Miss Ungermeyer had heard enough. She pulled out a megaphone. "Attention, parents!" she shouted. "SHUT YOUR PIEHOLES!"

That stopped the chatter. Lizzie wasn't sure if she should laugh or run away now, while she still could.

"I am on a mission to drag your progeny to

thirty-one historically significant Roman landmarks in two weeks," she said. "When these back-talking miscreants return to you, they will have dipped their toes into a lake of culture before assuming their destiny folding shirts at the outlet mall."

Nobody said a word. Except for Matt. "She seems nice," he said with a grin.

Miss Ungermeyer cast her laserlike scrutiny on Lizzie and the students around her. "Many . . . actually, *most* of your classmates opted for a thirty-six-hour bus ride to Waterslide Wonderland and a week stay at the Water Wonder Motor Inn." Her voice dripped sarcasm. "But you, who are not mouth-breathing trailer trash, will get to experience the delights of *La Città Eterna*."

Everyone stared, uncomprehending.

"Rome—the Eternal City," Miss Ungermeyer explained. "Did no one read the info packet?"

All the students scrambled to open their packets. Gordo leaned close to Lizzie. "Watch and learn," he whispered, then raised his hand. "Miss Ungermeyer, I just want to let you know that I'm looking forward to this exciting and academically enriching trip."

Their future principal narrowed the full force of her gaze on Gordo. Lizzie realized that her best friend had seriously stepped in it.

"Name?" Miss Ungermeyer barked at Gordo.

"David Gordon."

Miss Ungermeyer scribbled in a little pad. "David Gordon, sneaky brownnoser with hidden agenda."

Gordo blanched. "But—"

"All of you, embark on the plane NOW!" roared Miss Ungermeyer. "STAT! LET'S MOVE!"

Lizzie wasn't sure exactly what happened after that. Her mother pawed at her, tearfully babbling away. By the time Lizzie managed to pull free and say good-bye to everybody, she was swept into the wave of students heading excitedly to Gate B16.

They stood in line to board their flight. "Hey," said a voice in Lizzie's ear. Ethan Craft draped one arm across her shoulders and the other across Gordo's. "We're going to the land where they invented spaghetti!"

Lizzie couldn't hold back a grin. And the best part was, Kate and all her blow-drying, teeth-whitening addict friends who'd be ragging on her for messing up graduation went to Waterslide Wonderland!

That happy thought suddenly burst into flames as another voice said, "How many Lizzies does it take to screw in a lightbulb?" It was Kate. "I don't know," she answered herself merrily, "but it only takes *one* to screw up a graduation!"

Of course, she didn't go to Waterslide Wonderland. She melts when water touches her.

Fourteen hours later, Lizzie, Gordo, and their classmates trudged out of the plane and entered Rome's Fiumicino Airport. Lizzie hoped she didn't look as bad as she felt, because she felt like crud and a half. The first two hours in the plane had been so much fun! The rest had made her feel like a lemon in a juice press. "Did we have actual seats, or did we fly in the overhead compartments?" she asked Gordo, wondering why her tongue felt like a wadded-up sock.

In reply, Gordo sniffed his armpit. "Eww. Don't come near me."

"Like anyone would ever," Kate chirped.

Lizzie gawked at her ex-best friend in

disbelief. How did Kate do it? She looked perfect. Pristine. As energetic as ever. "That's not the outfit she wore on the plane," Lizzie whispered to Gordo. But—how? Her carry-on bag was microscopic!

Kate strutted past Lizzie like a peacock. "People who haven't traveled—*shouldn't*."

Half an hour later, everybody was packed in a yellow tour bus that swept through the streets of Rome. The late afternoon sun shone brightly on the beautiful city, but Lizzie couldn't focus on anything. Despite the fact that she'd had little to do during the flight except sleep, she still felt totally exhausted. And what time was it, anyway? Shouldn't it be dark out?

The bus stopped, and everybody filed out. Like tired sheep after a long day's graze, the students followed Miss Ungermeyer into the lobby of a small, but completely charming hotel and, at her signal, gathered around.

"Welcome to the Hotel Cambini," said Miss Ungermeyer. She continued to talk as she took a quick head count. "Lest you think there are more of you and less of me and therefore you will be able to pull anything over me, think again. In addition to my being smarter and faster—I have enlisted help." She indicated a short man with a dark mustache, wearing a wide smile, who stood attentively nearby. "The assistant manager of this hotel, Giorgio Averni, was a commander in the Italian navy and is as on top of his game as I am on mine. Giorgio, feel free to brief my students on security procedures here at the hotel."

"We serve at five the cookies," Giorgio said in a heavy Italian accent.

Lizzie shook her head. Huh? Before she could puzzle it out, Miss Ungermeyer cried, "Room assignments!" Gordo and Ethan were paired up. Then she turned to Lizzie. "Lizzie McGuire, seeing as how Margaret Chan was unable to make the trip, you'll be rooming with—"

Okay, I am *not* under any circumstances sharing a room with–"

KATE?! Lizzie couldn't believe her rotten luck when Miss Ungermeyer announced her sentence. But shortly thereafter, as Kate claimed the bed by the window in the room the two girls were forced to share, the horrible reality was undeniable.

"Lizzie," said Kate brightly, "seeing as we're roomies now and we're going to be spending all this time together, I want you to know that I understand you want to put all that really embarrassing stuff behind you and just move on and have a fresh start."

Lizzie continued to stare at Kate, but now she felt less horror and more curiosity. "You do?" she asked in disbelief.

"Yes," said Kate. "I understand your dream. It's a big dream. It's a huge dream. And you can't do it alone. In fact, I don't think you can do it at all." Kate smiled sadly. "Let it go."

Lizzie felt her cheeks go red and wondered how the universe could be so cruel. So often. To *her*.

Good old Gordo came to her rescue. That evening, he took Lizzie up a flight of stairs he'd investigated earlier. Lizzie climbed step after step and suddenly found herself greeted by a thousand twinkling lights. The stairs led them to the rooftop of the hotel.

"Pretty cool, huh?" Gordo asked her.

"Wow," Lizzie replied. "So cool." And it was. Rome lay below her, glittering with lights, basking in the amber glow of twilight. She decided to make a resolution. "You know something? I'm not going to let Kate Sanders get to me. In fact, promise me something."

"Anything," Gordo said.

"Promise me we'll have adventures. This is our chance to start over—to do anything we want to do."

Gordo seemed to like that idea. He cocked his head, smiling. "Yeah, I know. Adventures. You're right. You and me. Deal. I need to, because when I get home I'm supposed to go to chemistry camp." He saw the look on Lizzie's face. "I kid you not."

"You know what's really frightening?" Lizzie asked him. "I think my mom signed me up for that, too." She looked out at the amazing scene before her and smiled. They might never have such an opportunity again. "We better get busy!"

CHAPTER 4

Half a world away, trouble was brewing.

Matt sat at his computer, studying a Web site about Rome. Melina, his friend and partner in crime, leaned over his shoulder. "I don't know what catastrophe's going to happen in Rome," Matt said, "but with Lizzie there, something will."

"What precisely are you going to do with that information?" Melina asked. "Just give it away like you did with the graduation video?"

Matt thought he was crafty and conniving. But compared to Melina, he was an amateur. "Hey, she was really freaked out by that," he said, smiling.

Melina didn't return the grin. "And you have *what* to show for it?"

Matt shrugged. It was a good point. "The pride of a job well done?"

"Try buying a PlayStation 2 with pride of a job well done." Melina smacked him. "Matt, Matt, Matt, we've been over this before. Cash up front. *Good Morning America*—news. No cash. Jerry Springer—entertainment. Cash."

As Matt realized the truth of Melina's words, Mrs. McGuire poked her head through the doorway. "Melina, are you staying for supper?"

"I'd love to, Mrs. McGuire," Melina answered, sweet as sugar. "We'll need extra energy to work on our summer reading list."

"Oh!" Mrs. McGuire said in delight. "In that case, I'll make brownies." She smiled and left, closing the door behind her.

Melina immediately snapped back. "I've said it before," she told Matt. "You're weak! Weak! Don't do anything without me first!"

Matt looked at Melina in awe. "You *rock*!" he said.

The next morning, Miss Ungermeyer woke her sheep early and herded them to their first historical site: the Trevi Fountain.

Lizzie was truly impressed. The fountain was huge, sculptured from marble, and so detailed that Lizzie felt she could study it for hours and still not be able to take it all in. Miss Ungermeyer had already told them the basic facts, such as the names of the architects (Pietro da Cortona and Gian Lorenzo Bernini); and the fact that it had taken more than one hundred years to finish and that it was done in the baroque style ("If it ain't baroque, don't fix it!" Lizzie couldn't help thinking). All the bigger-than-life figures were awe-inspiring, but the most magnificent was Neptune, who dominated the whole thing as he steered a chariot drawn by two incredible sea horses.

"Throughout history, people have come from around the world to put coins in the Trevi Fountain," Miss Ungermeyer was saying now. "Those people are suckers, because you make your own luck in the world. Moving on." She started to herd her sheep away.

Lizzie hung back with Gordo. She handed him a euro coin. "Forget what she says—make a wish."

Gordo took the coin thoughtfully. "I'm in Rome with my best friend. I'm good." He handed it back. "You make one."

Lizzie closed her eyes, squeezing the coin in her hand. Then she tossed it into the water. Opening her eyes, she watched the coin slowly sink to the bottom, sparkling in the sunlight.

Satisfied, she turned to go and almost bumped into a young man who was staring at her as if he were seeing a ghost. "Isabella?" he asked, his Italian accent making the word sound positively poetic.

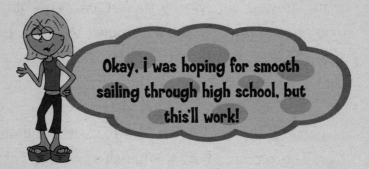

Okay, i was hoping for smooth sailing through high school, but this'll work!

Lizzie stared at the young man. Oh, boy, was he cute! "Huh . . . ?" she said.

"I am sorry," said the young man. "You look exactly like a friend of mine."

"No stragglers!" shouted Miss Ungermeyer. "We're moving!"

A huge mountain of a man standing near the young man tapped his watch. "Paolo. We have to get to your photo shoot." And so, both Lizzie and Paolo were pulled in the same direction. Lizzie's group was headed for the gelato store. The big man tried to steer Paolo to his photo shoot, which was across the street, but Paolo headed straight toward Lizzie, who ended up standing outside the store with Gordo.

"I don't mean to bother you," Paolo said. "I am Paolo, Paolo Valisari."

"Lizzie McGuire," Lizzie said, feeling awkward and transfixed at the same time. "And this is my friend Gordo."

"Hey," said Gordo.

"This is my friend Sergei." Paolo turned to the huge man next to him. "Sergei, doesn't she look like—"

Before he could finish, a crowd of Italians suddenly surged toward Lizzie and Paolo. "Isabella!" they cried, smiling and waving eagerly at them. "Paolo! Isabella!"

"What?" Lizzie cried, confused. "No, I—" But her words were lost in a babble of Italian. These people obviously thought she was somebody else, some Isabella person.

Paolo seemed to think the whole thing was amusing. He watched as Italians kissed Lizzie's hand and posed with her as friends took photos. An older woman handed her an enormous wheel of Parmesan cheese.

"Um. No. I couldn't," Lizzie protested.

Gordo looked up, and suddenly it all made sense. He nudged Lizzie, and she saw it, too. It was a billboard. Whoa, Paolo was on it! Double whoa—*so was she!* Or, rather, someone who looked just like her, only with dark hair. Lizzie figured out that the billboard was a music CD ad for *Paolo and Isabella,* obviously Italian pop stars.

"Wow, she really does look like me," Lizzie said.

"Except for the hair, you could be twins," replied Paolo, giving Lizzie a dazzling smile. "Isabella is my singing partner, and you are like her sister. Like two pods in a pea." He gazed at her, and the amazement in his eyes made Lizzie's knees go weak. "Can I see you again? Maybe tomorrow?"

"I don't think so. . . ." Lizzie blurted, wondering if she'd gone mad.

"Go," the ever loyal Gordo told her. "I'll cover for you."

"No," Lizzie said. "I can't. I'm with my school."

The sound of Miss Ungermeyer's voice pierced the air. "Head check!" Lizzie started to move toward her classmates, knowing that she'd be in real trouble if Miss Ungermeyer caught her this far away from the group.

Paolo followed her, speaking quickly. "Forgive me if I embarrassed you. It is just that some people, when they come to Rome, they want to . . . find adventure."

Lizzie paused. Did someone say—adventure? Then she shook her head. "It's okay," she said, holding up her wheel of Parmesan. "I got some cool cheese."

Did you just say *cool cheese*?!

Sergei turned to Paolo. "Paolo, we must go."

"Lizzie?" Paolo said.

"Yes?" replied Lizzie.

"If you change your mind," Paolo said, "I will meet you at Trevi Fountain tomorrow morning at nine. If you do not come—"

Miss Ungermeyer shouted, "Gordon! McGuire! Did you not hear me say HEAD CHECK?"

"She makes me very scared," Paolo said.

"Join the club," Gordo said, nodding.

Paolo grabbed Lizzie's hand. *"Ci vediamo,"* he said.

"What does that mean?" Lizzie asked.

"We will see each other," Paolo replied, kissing her hand.

A member of the Italian paparazzi caught the moment with his camera. *Flash!*

Matt stared at his computer screen in confusion. "Whoa!" he cried. "That girl looks freakishly like my sister!" Through the wonder of the Internet, the photograph of Lizzie and Paolo had been posted in cyberspace within hours of its being taken.

Melina, as usual, smacked Matt on the back

of the head. "Zoom! Zoom!" she ordered.

Matt obeyed. The picture on the screen got bigger and bigger until it fixed on the heart-shaped necklace hanging around the girl's neck.

"Another freakish coincidence!" Matt said. "She has the same necklace as my sister!"

Melina scowled at him. "Why do we even pretend you're in charge?" She pushed Matt out of his chair and sat down, tapping away at the keyboard. "Let's see what this says. 'Isabella goes blond! Italian pop duo Paolo and Isabella wowed the crowd outside a gelato shop near the Trevi Fountain, showing off Isabella's new blond hair.' Do you know what this means?" she asked.

Matt put two and two together as he picked himself up off the floor. "They must think Lizzie's this famous singer!" he said. "If I show this to my mom, Lizzie will get so busted!"

Annoyed, Melina almost smacked him again. But instead, she leaned back in her chair. "You know something? I'm tired," she said. "You just don't see the big picture."

"Well, that's as big as my screen will go," Matt said.

Melina sighed. "If you show this to your mother, it's worth *nothing*." She picked up a leather file case labeled LIZZIE BLACKMAIL to remind Matt of the precious loot inside: Polaroid photos, DVDs, videotapes, and a weird stuffed pig—all official documentation of embarrassing moments throughout Lizzie's life. "But if you show *this* to the Italian tabloids," Melina went on, "we will be rolling in cash, my friend."

A light of realization dawned in Matt's eyes. "Interesting," he said. "*We?*"

Melina nodded. "Sixty percent to me. Forty to you. For giving you the idea. And because I can kick your butt and take what I want, anyway."

Matt smiled. "Listen, Melina," he said, "by this time tomorrow, you're not going to be able to come over to my house and bat me around anymore, because I'll be eating real pizza in Rome, Italy, Europe!"

Melina patted his face tenderly. "I'll miss you," she cooed.

CHAPTER 5

That night in the hotel courtyard, Lizzie and Gordo spent some quality time together—researching Paolo and Isabella. Lizzie had purchased one of their CDs and was listening to it on her Discman while Gordo flipped through an Italian teen mag. He couldn't read the words, of course, but the pictures were telling him plenty. Namely, that Paolo and Isabella were hot, hot, hot.

"You know," Lizzie said, pointing to the

CD case, "these guys aren't bad. I mean, if you're into Alanis Morissette-y alternative, dark, like, brooding, I-never-go-out-in-the-sunlight-my-life-is-a-black-hole-of-depression kind of stuff, then you'd think they suck, but for the driving-around-in-the-car-putting-on-lip-gloss-with-the-top-down-loving-life kind of a thing, they're good. Listen."

She held out half of the headset so that Gordo could listen, too. He and Lizzie were practically cheek to cheek, and being in such close proximity to his best friend was making Gordo a little uncomfortable. But definitely not uncomfortable enough for him to move away. "Not bad," Gordo said after a moment. "Do you use scented soap?"

Lizzie blinked. "What?"

Gordo changed the subject—quickly. "Never mind."

Lizzie shrugged. "So what do you think? I

mean, this absolutely perfect guy who just happens to be a rock star picks me out of a crowd because I look like his singing partner"—she glanced at a picture of Isabella in Gordo's magazine—"which, weirdly enough, I kind of do. And now he wants to take me to lunch."

Gordo flipped the magazine page, not looking at her. "So, go."

"I'd have to sneak away."

"So?"

"I'm Lizzie McGuire," Lizzie said, as if that were some kind of curse. "I'm physically incapable of sneaking."

Gordo put his magazine down. "Weren't you the one who said we were going to have adventures?"

"Yeah, *we*," said Lizzie. "*We* were going to have adventures."

"Lizzie, we *will* have adventures," Gordo

replied. "You just have dibs on the first one."

"Okay, just as long as we don't do anything that gets us tossed on a plane home by Miss Ungermeyer," Lizzie said.

A thoughtful expression crossed Gordo's face. He finally looked at Lizzie, his eyes full of sympathy and concern. "Lizzie, are you feeling okay?"

Lizzie thought he'd gone nuts. "What? I feel fine."

Gordo shook his head and placed a hand on her forehead. "I don't know. You feel flushed."

Lizzie finally got it. She grinned. Good old Gordo!

Bright and early the next morning, Lizzie was still lying in bed while everybody else was up and getting dressed. Miss Ungermeyer called in a Dr. Comito, who spent a good fifteen minutes checking Lizzie over.

"Is this girl sick, or isn't she?" Miss Ungermeyer finally demanded.

"She doesn't have a fever, and yet she is in bed," said Dr. Comito. "Ask yourself why a beautiful young girl on her first visit to Rome, probably seeking adventure, wants to lie in bed all day? She is ill."

"I heard she fell down at graduation and made a complete fool of herself," Miss Ungermeyer said without a single trace of human compassion. "You think that could have something to do with it?"

"I saw that on CNN," Dr. Comito said. "It's possible. Often the nervous system collapses after that type of utter humiliation."

CNN? Does this mean the president knows?

Miss Ungermeyer gestured at Lizzie as if she were a math problem that needed to be solved. "What do you recommend, *il dottore?*"

"This young woman should stay in bed," the good doctor decided, and he scribbled on his prescription pad. "She must also eat two apricots."

"For digestion?" asked Miss Ungermeyer.

"No, they are in season. Very delicious. Feel better, Signorina McGuire," he said as he left.

"Rest, McGuire," said Miss Ungermeyer. "It would be a shame to miss out on the adventure of Rome."

Right you are!

The minute Miss Ungermeyer left, Lizzie sprang out of bed, fully dressed.

Matt entered the kitchen to find his father painting a gnome, of all things, and his mother making a sandwich. "I found something on the Internet I think both of you should see," Matt announced gravely. "Since Lizzie's in Europe, I thought I'd do a little e-search on Italy. But what I found out is not so *e-assuring*. In fact . . . it may shock you." Pleased at the looks of concern that blossomed on his parents' faces, Matt placed several papers on the kitchen counter. Pie charts. He was rather proud of them. He'd spent all night on them.

"What are we looking at?" his mother asked, glancing at them.

"Maybe nothing," said Matt ominously. "Maybe something. When polled, seventy-four percent of Italian teenaged boys said they would most like to date *American girls*."

Mr. McGuire picked up a chart and closely

examined it. "Son, you don't have to worry about your sister. She's well chaperoned. Miss Ungermeyer's there."

"Yeah, she's what?" Matt responded. "Five one? Five two?

Mr. McGuire glanced at his wife. "Honey?"

Matt's mother turned to her son. "Wait a minute. Matt, as interesting as this is, where are you taking it?"

Begin Phase Two! Matt looked down at his shoes. "You caught me," he said in his best poor-little-me voice. "I'll deny I ever said this but—I miss my sister. There. Now you know." Both of his parents were looking at him with genuine surprise. "I know I rag on her all the time," Matt continued, amazed by his own brilliant acting talents, "but now that she's not here, I . . . I feel so alone!"

Mrs. McGuire drew her son into her arms. "Honey, you don't have to make fake pie charts. You can always come to us with the truth."

Inspired, Matt decided to hug his mom tightly. She hugged back harder. Excellent!

"I know that now, Mommy," he said. "But it's hard. I miss her so much!" Heck, why not? He faked a sob. It sounded good. He kept doing it.

Mrs. McGuire looked at her husband over her sobbing son's head. "I can't believe I ever let you talk me into letting Lizzie go on that trip," she said.

"I'll dig out the passports," Mr. McGuire told her.

Matt grinned. Victory!

Later that morning, Lizzie found herself standing at Trevi Fountain. It had taken all her navigation skills to use the map and follow the signs, but she'd made it. And there was Paolo, just like he had promised. He was giving some children coins to throw into the fountain. He looked up and spotted Lizzie. "I had them all wish for you to come," he said, pointing to the kids.

Lizzie nervously checked her watch. "I don't have much time," she told him, hating herself for having to say those words. Why did Reality have to poke its nose into everything?

"Wait," Paolo said. "I have to show you something." He led her down a side street and stopped beside a brand-new, gleaming red Vespa.

"Wow!" said Lizzie.

Paolo smiled. "I just thought you should see Rome the way the Romans do."

Lizzie looked at the motor scooter, then at Paolo—and the truth hit her. "You knew I would come?"

"I *hoped* you would."

Lizzie couldn't help but press the issue. "Because I remind you of your girlfriend?"

Paolo didn't answer at first. He put on his helmet and climbed onto the Vespa. "You remind me of Isabella," he admitted, "but she's no longer my girlfriend." He held out a second helmet.

Lizzie didn't even hesitate. She took it.

Touchdown!

The next two hours were like a dream. Lizzie saw Rome from the back of a handsome pop star's Vespa, the wind whipping at her hair, her arms wrapped around Paolo's waist— and Sergei following in his car. Oh, well, so it wasn't *completely* perfect.

Or was it? Winding through quaint streets

and wide avenues, dodging crowds and scattering flocks of ever present pigeons, they drove from one marvel to the next: the Pantheon, temple to all the ancient Roman gods; Piazza Navona; Piazza Farnese. It was all breathtaking.

Paolo's little Vespa could squeeze through almost any traffic jam—and Rome seemed to be one big traffic jam—but at one point they got stuck behind a truck trying to turn around on a narrow street. Lizzie took the opportunity to talk to Paolo. "Paolo, can I ask you something?"

Paolo turned around. "If you want an autograph, you'll have to pay like everyone else," he joked.

Lizzie swatted at him playfully.

"Okay, for you, it is free," he said.

Lizzie laughed. "Is this really happening? Or is it just part of one big really weird dream I'm having?"

"If you are dreaming," said Paolo, "then I am dreaming it, too."

Lizzie nodded. "Okay, next question."

"*Sì, carina?*" replied Paolo.

Lizzie smiled. "Say that again."

"What—*sì, carina?*" Paolo repeated.

"Yes," said Lizzie happily. "So, I know your life is just a little bit different than mine. . . ." After a moment, she added, "Well, like, several universes different . . . but doesn't your friend Sergei get tired of following us around in that car all the time?"

"Actually, Sergei is my bodyguard," Paolo told her. "There is not a Vespa big enough to hold him."

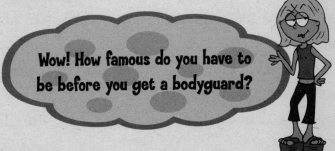

Wow! How famous do you have to be before you get a bodyguard?

"So you see," Paolo continued, "between me and Sergei, you will always be safe."

Paolo's words made Lizzie feel warm all over. But a chill ran down her spine the next moment when a yellow tour bus pulled up next to them. Lizzie recognized every face in every window. It was the Ungermeyer Express!

Inside the bus, Gordo glanced out the window and almost choked. He leaped up and scrambled to the front of the bus where Miss Ungermeyer was sitting.

"Miss Ungermeyer!" he called.

Miss Ungermeyer shot him a disapproving glance. "Mr. Gordon," she lectured, "this bus could be in motion again at any moment. By standing, you are violating rule number two of bus safety."

WHOMP! The bus pulled forward and Gordo lost his balance and crashed to the floor. He crawled forward and pulled himself into the seat beside Miss Ungermeyer. "What's rule number one?" he asked, wincing in pain.

"Never keep a pen in your back pocket," she replied.

Gordo twisted around, and sure enough, a blossom of ink was spreading on his posterior.

"I didn't think I had a pen in my back pocket," he said.

"So, maybe it's spinal fluid," Miss Ungermeyer said dismissively. "Take your seat."

Gordo looked out the window. Lizzie was still there. "Didn't we just pass the Castel Sant'Angelo?" He pointed out the window on the non-Lizzie side of the bus.

"Yes," said Miss Ungermeyer. "What about it?"

"Well," Gordo said, thinking fast, "I notice it's not on our itinerary."

"That's correct." Presuming the conversation

finished, Miss Ungermeyer resumed looking out the Lizzie-side window.

Gordo gulped. "Well, shouldn't it be?" he cried. "I mean, it was a papal residence, and it contains frescoes from artists influenced by the school of Raphael."

He must have sounded a little too passionate, because Miss Ungermeyer had a suspicious gleam in her eye. "What are you up to, Mr. Gordon?"

"Nothing," said Gordo. "I just felt while in Rome we should be exposed to as much Renaissance Raphaelite work typified by chiaroscuro and Hellenic mythical imagery as humanly possible." He dared a glance out the window and saw Paolo zip the Vespa through a crack in the traffic jam. "But you da boss!" he finished.

Whew! Mission accomplished. Gordo stood to return to his seat, violating rule number two yet again. *WHOMP!*

Miss Ungermeyer stared down at him, her eyes narrowed. "You're on the list, Mr. Gordon. The list is not a place you want to be."

CHAPTER 6

Not long after Lizzie's narrow escape from the Tour Bus of Doom, she and Paolo were strolling through the Campo de' Fiori, a plaza filled with shops and tourists. As if to emphasize the name of the place—which translates to "field of flowers"—a *fiorista* held up a big yellow rose from his vendor cart. "Ciao, Isabella!" he called to Lizzie.

"I'm not—" Lizzie began, but Paolo nudged her.

"In Italy we say *grazie*," he informed her.

"*Grazie,*" Lizzie said to the flower vendor, and took the rose.

The vendor smiled at her. "*Prego!*" he said, and returned to his cart.

They resumed walking. "Paolo," Lizzie asked, breathing in the elegant perfume of the rose, "do you still love her?"

The question seemed to take the young pop star by surprise. "Isabella?" he said slowly. "Of course, I still love her . . . but like a sister."

Lizzie tried to hide her smile. Great! Paolo was a free man! "Why did you break up?" she asked him, trying to sound nonchalant.

"Ah . . . it's complicated." Paolo stopped walking and faced her. "I mean, okay, sure we've been voted pop duo of the year *again*, and, yes, our last two CDs went double platinum, but . . . I want to do more serious music. And when I told Isabella, she said flat out no. No! So I told her that's it, this is our last CD together. She's really upset, and I feel really bad about that, but what about me? I mean, I need to grow as an artist, you know? So yesterday, when I saw you, and saw how all those people thought you were Isabella, I . . . I . . ." He sighed. "I don't know. I had this crazy idea that you could help me."

Lizzie wanted to ask him how, but Paolo took her hand and led her to a café.

"Come on, Paolo," Lizzie finally said as they sat down at a table. "How crazy could it be? Just tell me."

"Okay," he said. "Isabella and I are supposed to present an award together at the International Music Video Awards."

"The IMVA?" Lizzie said in amazement. "Cool! I mean, cool for regular people. Like me. I guess for you it's like work."

"No, it's cool for me, too. You get nice gift

baskets, and you get to see Courtney Love fight with Mariah Carey over dressing rooms." He leaned closer and whispered, "Courtney is very strong." As Lizzie chuckled, he continued, "But Isabella has refused to go, and now the record company is threatening to take her to court. If we don't fulfill our contract, Isabella will be ruined."

"Well, what about you?" Lizzie asked.

"For me it is no problem," Paolo said with a dismissive wave of his hand. "I write the music. They just come to me, I can't stop them. La, la, la, la, la! See? I can go solo. But Isabella . . ." Again he leaned in close to whisper. "She needs the help to sing."

It took a moment for Lizzie to understand what he meant. When she did, she blurted out, "You mean Isabella *lip-synchs*?" And she said it way too loudly.

"Shhh!" said Paolo. "Please," he continued,

"You must promise me you'll speak of this to no one. Think of what it would do to Isabella's career." He gazed across the table at Lizzie, his eyes full of desperation. "When I saw you, that's when I had my crazy idea that you could pretend to be Isabella for one night and present the award with me."

"Present an award?" Lizzie squeaked. "Onstage?"

"*Sì,*" said Paolo. "For Isabella . . . so she does not get sued."

"In front of an *audience*? I'm not good in front of crowds," Lizzie said, feeling lame. "I could *never* do that."

"Of course, you can do it." Paolo took her hand and kissed it. "You are *magnifica*!"

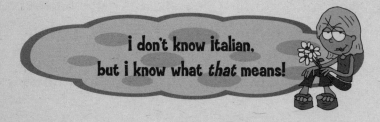

i don't know italian, but i know what *that* means!

Paolo released her hand. "Don't worry, *carina*. I would never ask you to do this crazy thing. It would mean that you would have to be someone else for a couple days, a pop star wearing different makeup and clothes, having the entire world at your fingertips. It is far too much to ask."

Well, when he put it *that* way, it all made so much sense! Lizzie took a deep breath. "You don't have to ask. If it will help you and your ex-girlfriend Isabella, then I'll do it."

Paolo smiled. *"Grazie."*

Lizzie smiled back. *"Prego,"* she answered.

That night, after she was sure Miss Ungermeyer was asleep in her room, Lizzie tiptoed to Gordo's room and knocked softly. When he opened the door, Lizzie slipped inside, relieved to see that Gordo's roommate, Ethan, wasn't there. She had so much to tell Gordo! She started to fill him in.

"Wait. You, Lizzie McGuire, are presenting an award at the IMVA with Paolo?" Gordo asked incredulously.

"No, me, *Isabella* with Paolo," Lizzie corrected him. "It's a long story, but I'm doing it because the real Isabella won't."

Gordo was still trying to grasp the idea. "You're actually going to get up onstage in front of all those people?"

Lizzie nodded. "That's what's so great about it—I won't be me! It's all Paolo's idea to help Isabella because he still loves her . . . like a sister," she quickly added. "He's so amazing! I mean, for someone who's famous and who is used to getting everything he wants, he's so—I don't know—kind."

Gordo frowned. "For real," he said, "that's a lot to say about someone just knowing them one day."

"I know," said Lizzie. "But I just feel like I've known him my whole life. Haven't you ever felt that way about someone?"

Had he? Of course he had—Lizzie! But Gordo didn't say anything.

"Anyway," Lizzie continued. "I just wanted to thank you for making me go today. I never would have had the most magical day of my life if it hadn't been for you."

"Wow—it was that great?" Gordo asked uncomfortably.

Lizzie kissed Gordo on the forehead. "You're such a good friend."

Stunned, Gordo just stood there and watched her leave. That's when Ethan came out of the bathroom. "The sting," Ethan said, watching Lizzie's exit. "You want a little mano a mano?"

Gordo looked at his roommate, his brow furrowing. "See, one of the many reasons we're not friends is I never have any idea what you're talking about."

Ethan didn't seem to be insulted. He just said, "Some dudes get the approach. Others get the sting. That Italian dude, he's big-time approach."

Gordo tried to find meaning somewhere in those words and failed. "I actually feel my brain turning to goo," he muttered.

"Embrace the sting," Ethan went on. "That's what you're vibing here from Lizzie."

Now Gordo sensed Ethan's meaning. "Wait a minute. You're saying I'm *jealous* of Paolo?"

Ethan nodded somberly. "Word."

"Well that would mean that I like her more than just a friend, and . . ." Gordo trailed off.

"What do you mean, you and I have trouble communicating, bro?" Ethan asked with a smirk.

"Well, you're wrong," Gordo finished. Ethan *was* wrong, wasn't he?

CHAPTER 7

"Not up to toughing it out in the streets with us, Miss McGuire?" Miss Ungermeyer asked. She was standing, once more, above a bedridden Lizzie McGuire. Lizzie had given the performance of a lifetime trying to struggle out of bed. She managed to fail quite well, she thought.

"I could try, Miss Ungermeyer," Lizzie said hoarsely.

Miss Ungermeyer shook her head. "No, I

just hate that you're being denied the cultural experience of being in a foreign country. You missed seven points of historical significance yesterday."

"It's killing me, too, Miss Ungermeyer," Lizzie said sadly.

Miss Ungermeyer gave her a thin-lipped smile. "Which is why I've brought something to ease your pain."

Lizzie brightened a bit. "That's so thoughtful of you."

"Since your body obviously doesn't have the strength, your mind can do the wandering instead." Miss Ungermeyer held up a thick textbook. *"The Rise and Fall of the Roman Empire.* I want one report on the rise, one on the fall." She caught the brief expression of horror that crossed Lizzie's face. "You don't have a problem with that, do you, Miss McGuire?"

Lizzie forced a sweet but sickly smile. "Of course not. I mean, what else do I have to do?"

Soon Lizzie was once again on the back of the Vespa, cruising the streets of Rome. Paolo guided the little vehicle to the Via Condotti and parked it.

Lizzie took one look at the street and felt her jaw go slack. Beyond a doubt, this was the Rodeo Drive of Rome. Feeling like a pauper among princes, she followed Paolo as he began to stroll along, followed by the ever vigilant Sergei in his Mercedes convertible.

"I am so grateful for your help," Paolo said. "You are doing a very kind thing for Isabella."

Lizzie smiled. "Where are we?" she asked.

"The Via Condotti," Paolo answered. "It is one of the most expensive shopping streets in the world. We must find you the perfect dress for the awards night."

"Um, Paolo, I can't afford to shop here," Lizzie said. "I can't afford to *walk* here!"

"Do not worry about money," Paolo said with a smile.

"Why would I?" Lizzie asked. "I don't have any."

Lizzie stopped in front of a ritzy-looking store called Prada. "Listen," she said firmly, "you've been so nice to me and everything, but I can't let you buy me stuff. I wouldn't feel right."

"But it is not me, Lizzie," said Paolo. "It is the record company. *They* pay."

"Get out!" she said in astonishment.

"And you can buy as much as you want and you get to keep it all!" Paolo said.

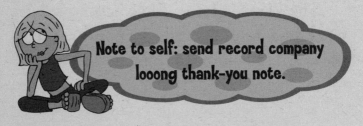

Note to self: send record company looong thank-you note.

Lizzie let happy little dollar signs dance past her eyes for a moment. Then, with a huge smile, she charged into the store.

Lizzie's Splurge of the Century was over all too quickly. One minute she was stepping into the store; the next minute Sergei's car was jammed with packages, boxes, and bags. Lizzie's happiness would have been absolutely complete if she'd known that, far, far away, Kate Sanders suddenly sat bolt upright in her bus seat, shouting, "Oh, my God, there's incredible shopping going on, and it doesn't involve me!"

Followed by Sergei in his now full car, Paolo next took Lizzie to the Franca DiMontecatini Designer Salon, one of the most expensive fashion studios in the world. Lizzie crossed the threshold and felt like she'd stepped onto Planet Chic. Loud technopop music played on hidden speakers. Two gorgeous models, dressed in Franca's creations, stopped to say hello to Lizzie.

"Ciao, Isabella!" said one.

"Oh, ciao!" Lizzie replied. She was getting better at this.

The second model stared at Lizzie's hair. "Your hair, the blond. So innocent! Who did it?"

"Uhh . . ." Lizzie began. "A lot of sun . . . on the island. It was a really, really sunny island."

The first model touched Lizzie's hair and turned to her model friend. "We must get sun, too."

The models kissed Lizzie and strolled off. Lizzie watched them go in awe. She turned to Paolo. "They. Are. So. Tall," she said.

"You see?" Paolo said to her. "They all want to be *you*."

Lizzie shook her head. "They want to be *Isabella*."

With a shrug, Paolo led her to a plush sofa. "Here, sit and I will get Franca. I'll just be a *momento*."

That was fine with Lizzie. The minute she sat down, salon employees bustled out of nowhere and offered her cookies, cappuccino, bottles of water, even Italian *tramezzini*—little sandwiches with the crusts cut off. Someone also brought her a telephone and a pile of fashion magazines. Paolo watched all this with amusement.

When Lizzie realized he was still there, she grinned up at him. "Take your time. I'll just be sitting here in heaven."

As Lizzie munched cookies and sipped cappuccino, her peers were herded to the Roman Forum by Miss Ungermeyer, who delighted in lecturing on Roman history, especially when she thought someone was actually listening.

"Hard as it is to imagine as we look at these crumbling ruins of the Forum, this was once the center of commerce, religion, and politics in ancient Rome," she told her sheep enthusiastically. "The Forum came into being around the sixth century B.C., and with it, a new urban culture was born. Those responsible for creating this unique gathering place were the Etruscans. Can anyone tell me which kings were in power during this time?"

Silence.

"That would be the *Etruscan* kings," Miss Ungermeyer said, disgusted that nobody had at least taken a stab at such an obvious question. "But who cares about dead Italian rulers when you've got four hundred channels of cable TV at home, right?" she added sarcastically.

Everyone muttered in agreement as Ethan raised his hand. "Is it time for the spaghetti?"

Kate frowned at him. "It's, like, nine in the morning."

"Yeah, so?" said Ethan. "You never had left-over spaghetti for breakfast?"

"I don't eat carbs," Kate replied coldly.

"And I suppose you never made a spaghetti sandwich?" Ethan went on.

"Sanders, Craft!" barked Miss Ungermeyer. "Separate!"

"Oh, we did, Miss Ungermeyer," Kate said. "And thank God."

At that, Miss Ungermeyer groaned and massaged her temples. "Education is wasted on the young," she grumbled, then said to the herd, "Why don't you attempt something more on your skill level and take a ten-minute shopping break while I choke down an espresso!"

The students fled to the souvenir stands. Gordo found himself saddled with Ethan, who was studying a little figurine of Michelangelo's *David*. "This dude definitely spent too much time working biceps and not enough abs," Ethan said critically. "Totally old school."

But Gordo wasn't listening. He was too busy watching two very cute Italian girls. Or rather, he was trying to see the cover of the magazine that one of them carried. On it was a photo of Paolo and Isabella.

Ethan followed Gordo's gaze and nodded approvingly. "Nice spot, bro. Watch and learn. The Closeout." He set his jaw and focused his blue eyes on the girls, striking his most rugged, tough-guy pose. To Gordo, it made Ethan look like he had indigestion, but the girls giggled. "Works every time," Ethan said.

Gordo still wasn't listening to him. "I've got to go talk to them," he said, and headed toward the girls.

"No, that's not how the Closeout works, bro," Ethan said. "They come to *us*!"

Gordo ignored him. "Ciao," he said to the girls. "Do you speak English?"

"Yes," said one girl, giving Gordo a once-over and frowning in disappointment. "It is your friend we like," she added heartlessly.

"Word," Gordo said.

"Is that his name?" asked another girl. "Word?"

"Yeah," Gordo replied. He had no time for this. "Hey, listen, you know these guys?" He pointed to the magazine cover.

"Paolo and Isabella?" said the first girl. "*Certo!*"

"Can you translate what this says?" Gordo asked her.

The second girl thought for a moment. "Only if you introduce us to your friend Word."

"Can I keep your magazine?"

"Deal."

The girl handed over the magazine, and Gordo escorted them over to Ethan.

"Hello, there," Ethan drawled, trying to look his sexiest.

"Ciao, Word," said one of the girls.

Confused, Ethan looked at Gordo.

Gordo just shrugged.

CHAPTER 8

Lizzie stood as Paolo, Franca DiMontecatini, and various assistants approached her. Lizzie wondered how she was going to communicate with the woman, not knowing that Paolo had convinced Franca that "Isabella" needed to practice her English. Franca held a Pomeranian dog wearing a diamond-studded collar. Lizzie took a closer look—were the dog's toenails painted pink? Why, yes, they were! The dog, not recognizing Lizzie, began barking at her.

"What! Have! You! Done?!" Franca exploded when she saw Lizzie. "You look like a *schoolgirl*!"

Everyone gasped. The dog continued to bark at Lizzie.

"What's wrong, Maximus?" Franca said. "It's Isabella. You love Isabella." But the dog obviously did not love Lizzie and barked even louder.

"Nice Maximus," Lizzie said nervously.

Franca looked at her dog. "Very odd," she said. She stared at Lizzie. "There is something . . . something very different about you. . . ."

"Rest," said Paolo. "The rest on the island did Isabella a world of good. She is transformed."

Franca stared at Lizzie unhappily. "Well, I can't put clothes on this!" She turned to her assistants. "Fix the hair! Fix the eyebrows! Fix the lips! Fix the ears!"

"The ears?" Lizzie said nervously.

"Jewelry," said Franca.

The next two hours passed in a blur. Lizzie's body was measured, her hair styled, her cheeks highlighted, her eyebrows tweezed, her nails manicured, her lashes curled, and her ears fixed. Lastly, she tried on clothes. Clothes, clothes, and more clothes. It was so much fun to be the center of attention! And the outfits were to die for. A cellophane dress. An electric dress. An inflatable dress. A pull-up dress. She tried on anything and everything, and still Franca urged her to try on more.

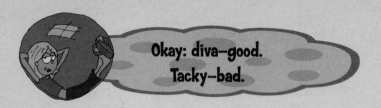

Okay: diva—good.
Tacky—bad.

Finally, however, she had enough. "None of these are me," she complained to Paolo as she struggled to stay upright in a pair of stiletto heels.

Paolo just laughed. "You're not supposed to be you."

"But if I'm supposed to go onstage, as Isabella, in front of a bunch of people, I need . . ."—what did she need?—"to be confident," Lizzie decided. "Which is, like, the thing I'm worst at."

"We are all the same that way," said Paolo.

"Not you," argued Lizzie.

"Yes, me, too," said Paolo. "And Isabella. It is how she works through her fears that makes her strong."

Lizzie considered this.

"For instance," said Paolo, "Isabella doesn't let Franca DiMontecatini tell her what to wear! *She* tells Franca!"

Lizzie blanched. "*Me* tell Franca DiMontecatini how I should dress?"

"*Sì*, Isabella," said Paolo, giving her a little push. "Test your strength. *Vai.*"

Lizzie tried to control the stilettos as she strode purposefully over to Franca. All she had to do was borrow Isabella's confidence, right? So, no Lizzie, no Lizzie, only Isabella, only Isabella . . .

Franca saw the look on Lizzie's face and spoke first. "You don't like my clothes."

"I love your clothes," Lizzie said honestly. "But I don't like your dressing me." As Franca's eyes bugged in disbelief, Lizzie went on, "I'm not your Barbie doll. I'm Isabella Parigi, and I dress myself. Choices! I need choices!" she said, divalike. Then, thinking maybe she had gone too far, she added, "please."

Franca nodded to her assistants, who disappeared and came out bearing bolts of fabric in different colors. Lizzie checked them out, then turned to Franca, pointing at two different fabrics. "I like these two," she said. "You pick."

Franca looked flattered. "This one," she said.

Lizzie was excited. "That's the exact color I wore to a spring formal, and Danny Kessler thought I—" She stopped.

Franca and her assistants were staring at her.

Lizzie panicked for a second. She'd blown her cover! Then inspiration hit. "Look at all of you!" she laughed. "You think I'm American!" Adopting an Italian accent, she added, "I am—how they say—awesome!"

Impressed, Franca positively beamed. "The island—you must go more often," she said.

* * *

An hour later, Lizzie was dancing with joy down the most famous set of steps in the world—the Scalinata di Spagna, or Spanish Steps.

Lizzie knew nothing of the rich history around her. Right now, she felt like a million bucks, and that was all that mattered. "Goodbye, Lizzie McGuire—hello, fabulous!" she sang to the world, doing a few cartwheels.

Paolo watched with satisfaction as a throng of teenaged Italian fans rushed toward the two of them. Now Lizzie showed no hesitation. She shook everyone's hands and posed for photos. A cute boy wanted her to autograph his arm. "L-i-z-" Lizzie started to write. Then she crossed it out and signed "Isabella." She kissed him on the cheek. He swooned.

i'm ready for my close-up now.

Staring at her fans, Lizzie got a little carried away. She turned to Sergei. "Sergei," she said. "I want you to get tickets for all my friends to come to the IMVA."

"All?" said Sergei.

"Yes," replied Lizzie. The fans cheered. Lizzie turned to Paolo. "Did I go too far?" she asked.

"Not far enough," Paolo replied. When Lizzie gave him a confused look, he pointed at the yellow school bus parked nearby. "Look!" he said.

Miss Ungermeyer and Lizzie's fellow students were at the Spanish Steps, too! Kate was filming cute Italian boys. "How come not one Roman guy has asked me out yet?" she complained.

Gordo rolled his eyes. Then he glanced at the steps and spotted Lizzie and Paolo. His eyes widened.

Kate had spotted Paolo, too, and could see a blond girl standing behind him. "Where's the zoom on this thing?" she muttered.

But before she could zoom in, the camera went black. Kate looked up. Gordo was standing right in front of her.

"Hello? Excuse me?" Kate said, annoyed.

"Oh. Sorry," said Gordo.

Miss Ungermeyer blew her whistle. "Spanish Steps HEAD CHECK!" she shouted. "Then back on the bus and back to the hotel! *Andiamo! Andiamo!*"

Lizzie saw the kids heading back to the bus. "Quick, let's go!" she cried to Paolo. "I gotta get back to the hotel before they do!"

She and Paolo ran up the stairs, disappearing into the crowd.

Gordo watched them go.

Making record time, Paolo drove his Vespa through traffic and got her to the Hotel

Cambini only moments before the bus arrived. While Paolo distracted Giorgio at the front desk, Lizzie tiptoed past and ducked into an elevator, rushed to her room, threw off her clothes, got into her pajamas, and ran the hair dryer against her forehead for a few seconds. Then she leaped into bed and pulled the covers up to her chin just as Kate and Miss Ungermeyer entered the room.

"Mom . . . ?" Lizzie croaked, hoping she sounded convincingly feverish.

Kate threw her a suspicious glare as Miss Ungermeyer put her hand on Lizzie's forehead. "Still a little warm. Miss Sanders, why don't you look after her?"

Kate practically gagged at the very concept. "Look after her? As in, do stuff for her? Miss Ungermeyer, why should I be punished? I'm not the one who's sick!"

Miss Ungermeyer sighed. "Next year, I'm

joining the mouth-breathers at Waterslide Wonderland," she grumbled, and left.

The second she was gone, Kate turned on Lizzie. "You are so busted. You've been out of this hotel room."

That was the last thing Lizzie expected to hear. "But how do you—?" Lizzie began.

"Please," Kate said. "Your eyebrows finally match. You have highlights." She yanked down the bedsheets. "Fresh manicure! I smelled the acetone the second I got off the elevator."

Lizzie felt like a mouse cornered by a big hungry cat. "But . . . but . . . you didn't rat me out to Miss Ungermeyer."

"Yet," said Kate. "Not until I figure out what's in it for me. Now spill, Dorkerella."

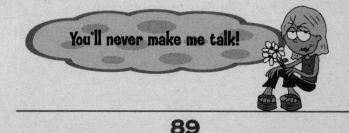

You'll never make me talk!

"I just want to know how this could happen," Kate said after she'd heard the whole story.

Lizzie sat on her bed, Kate sat on hers, and they stared at each other. "Well, part of it is genetics," Lizzie said. "Isabella and I do look a lot alike."

"No," said Kate, "I meant, how did *you* get *my* trip? How could Lizzie McGuire be living this fantasy, and I can't even get an Italian guy to buy me a slice of pizza?"

Lizzie called up her "Isabella confidence" and said, "Why don't you try being nice?"

Kate reacted as if she'd been slapped. "That's ridiculous! It's a well-known fact that never works with guys."

"Well, we're in another country," Lizzie reminded her. "Try something new."

Kate folded her arms. "I suppose you want me to keep this quiet."

"I'd appreciate that," Lizzie replied.

Kate laid out the deal. "I'll keep it quiet if you keep it quiet about my keeping it quiet. And when we get home, I'm the cool one again, and you turn back into a pumpkin."

Before Lizzie could reply, somebody knocked on the door. Kate opened it to reveal Gordo. "What do you want?" she asked him, frowning. "We're closed."

Gordo tried to look past her, but Kate blocked his view. "I just wanted to talk to Lizzie for a second."

"Okay," said Kate, and stepped aside. "Talk."

"Um. I was kind of thinking maybe out in the courtyard."

Kate smirked. "If it's about the bizarre parallel universe Italian-rock-star-Lizzie's-suddenly-a-diva-thing, I know all about it."

Gordo looked at Lizzie in disbelief.

"She figured it out," Lizzie confessed.

Gordo looked at Kate, impressed. "Evil *and* smart," he said. He held up the magazine he'd gotten from the Italian girls. "I thought you'd want to see this," he told Lizzie.

Lizzie stared at the photo of herself. "Oh, my God, I'm on the front page of a tabloid!"

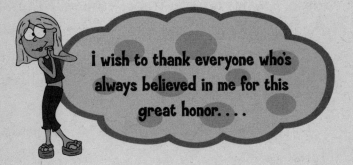

i wish to thank everyone who's always believed in me for this great honor....

"Know what this says?" Gordo asked her. "It says Paolo and Isabella are *singing* at the IMVA."

Lizzie grabbed the magazine out of Gordo's hands, feeling as if her heart had just turned to lead. "There's no way—"

"I had some Italian girl translate it," Gordo said. "Paolo didn't tell you?"

Lizzie looked up at her best friend, trying to reach for that "Isabella confidence," but it just wasn't there. "No . . ." she said in a tiny voice.

"Don't you think it's weird that he tried to hide it from you?" Gordo asked.

Lizzie refused to believe what Gordo was implying. "Maybe it's just a last-minute change."

"Aren't these things planned in advance?" Sensing that Lizzie was still skeptical, Gordo went on. "Forget it. If you just want to believe some guy, who you think you know after two days because he's an international superstar, really rich, and has good hair, be my guest." He walked out the door.

Lizzie and Kate sat in silence, digesting what Gordo had just said.

"There's got to be some mistake" was all

Lizzie could say. "Paolo is picking me up in a few minutes, so I'll talk to him." As if on cue, a car horn beeped outside. Lizzie hopped off her bed. "I gotta go."

"Don't worry, I'll cover for you in case Miss Ungermeyer does one of her psycho middle-of-the-night head checks," Kate said.

Kate? Being nice? *Again?* "I owe you," Lizzie told her ex-best friend.

"Duh," Kate replied.

CHAPTER 9

After sneaking out of the hotel lobby, Lizzie reached again for her newfound "Isabella confidence" as she strode up to Paolo's car. "Paolo, are we supposed to sing?" she asked him.

"Scusa?" said Paolo.

Don't speak to me in italian. it's too adorable.

"Are Paolo and Isabella supposed to *sing* at the awards?" Lizzie asked.

It was a moment before Paolo answered. *"Sì,"* he said simply.

"Sì?" Lizzie said, bewildered. "Why didn't you tell me?"

"I wanted to call," Paolo said, "but you told me not to telephone the hotel. Get in, I'll explain everything, but we must be going. I want to take you to Tivoli before the sun sets."

Lizzie got in the car. "Where's Sergei?" she asked the pop star.

"You're not the only one who sneaks off at night," Paolo said.

From his hotel room window, Gordo, deep in thought, watched the two zoom away.

Paolo drove Lizzie through the city and out into the Italian countryside.

"Isabella and I were going to sing," he

explained as he drove. "But after Isabella would not speak to me, I told the producers we refused to perform. I said that Isabella had throat problems."

The two arrived at Tivoli, and Paolo parked.

"So what happened?" Lizzie asked, as they strolled along a beautiful garden path. "What changed?"

"Isabella did," Paolo answered.

Lizzie was confused. "The real Isabella or the me Isabella?"

"You," said Paolo. "The reporters heard us speaking in front of the photo shoot and reported Isabella's voice was fine. And they said her English was very good, by the way. Then the record company called, and they were going to sue if we don't sing now."

"They're forcing you . . . us . . . to sing?" Lizzie asked.

"Don't worry, *carina*. I will make this

work." He gestured ahead of them. "Look."

Lizzie looked. At the far end of the path was the most incredible fountain she'd seen yet: the Canopus, an elaborate structure with statues and columns and even a waterfall. Paolo grabbed Lizzie's hand, and they ran toward the fountain, like two excited little kids. He led Lizzie underneath the fountain's waterfall.

"This is impossible," Lizzie said. "I could never sing in front of an audience. I don't even let my mom hear me in the shower."

"Lizzie, I'll teach you all you need to know," Paolo assured her.

"What's Isabella going to do if she sees me being her?" Lizzie asked.

"Ah, but she won't," Paolo replied. "She's off on an island, getting over me. Poor thing." He changed the subject. "Here is my contract. If you do not fulfill it, you can give me the sue." He placed his hand over his heart. "I, Paolo

Valisari, will never let my friend Lizzie McGuire be embarrassed."

"Really?" Lizzie said.

"*Carina*, hasn't everything I promised come to be?" he asked. "Everyone thinks you are Isabella. You are having the time of your life being someone else. You showed Franca DiMontecatini who was boss. Don't you trust that we can do the singing together?"

"I guess . . ." Lizzie said uncertainly.

Paolo grinned and dipped his hand into the fountain water, splashing her. "Well, don't!" he warned her with a laugh.

The cold water seemed to wash away all her fears. Lizzie laughed, too, and splashed Paolo back. So began a glorious water fight.

Later, when they arrived back in Rome, Paolo stopped at a piazza where there was a big fireworks show in progress. They got out of the car to watch.

"Beautiful," said Lizzie.

"Yes, you are," replied Paolo, staring at her.

Lizzie smiled. As Paolo took her hand, she thought she might melt right then and there.

Not far away, Gordo stood on the rooftop of the Hotel Cambini, watching the same fireworks display. In his hand he held a piece of amber that Lizzie had given him. As he quietly rolled it around, he couldn't stop thinking of her.

The next morning, Miss Ungermeyer led her sheep out early, as usual. Gordo followed the group as everyone crossed the hotel lobby, eager as ever to see the sights but wishing that Lizzie could be with him. She'd reported in "sick" again today. He was glad she was having fun, but all this sneaking around was dangerous, and the fact was . . . he missed her.

When he saw her peek out from under a pile of laundry in a maid's cart, he nearly had a heart attack. The maid obviously had no idea she was aiding in an escape plan, and Gordo managed to stay cool as she pushed her cart across the lobby and through a back exit.

"Halt!" Miss Ungermeyer suddenly said.

Gordo froze. Had she seen Lizzie? Did she know what was going on? She pulled a package out of her purse and headed toward the stairs. "I forgot to give McGuire these apricots," she explained.

Gordo rushed up the stairs and leaped in front of his future principal, blocking her way.

"Uh, yes," Gordo said. "I'm beginning to . . ." —he searched for something, anything, to say—"to agree with Ethan. We should eat more spaghetti."

From the lobby, Ethan called up, "You da man!"

Miss Ungermeyer got a very unpleasant gleam in her eye. "Mr. Gordon, is there some reason you don't want me to go upstairs?"

"Uh, no," replied Gordo. Then he tapped his watch. "But we should get moving—so much Roma . . . so little time-a."

But Miss Ungermeyer ignored him. "When I go upstairs, and I *will* go upstairs, will I find McGuire in bed?" she asked.

"Sure," said Gordo. "I mean, unless she's in the bathroom or something."

The gleam got even more unpleasant. "She's not sick, is she?"

"Sure, she is," said Gordo, starting to sweat.

"This has all been an elaborate ruse to sneak out of the hotel, hasn't it?"

Gordo felt his stomach twist into a knot. The jig was up. However, he could still salvage the situation. "Yes, it has," he blurted out. "I've been sneaking out every night."

Miss Ungermeyer stared at Gordo in disbelief. *"You?"*

Gordo nodded, trying to radiate guilt. "I'm glad I got it off my chest."

"You realize what this means?" Miss Ungermeyer said icily.

Gordo felt his future slipping away. "I should look elsewhere for a college recommendation?"

Miss Ungermeyer nodded once, curtly. "I had you pegged from day one, David Gordon. Sneaky, brownnoser with a hidden agenda. And now—busted!"

Gordo trudged up the stairs, part of him so very happy for having helped Lizzie, and part of him wishing he'd never come to Rome at all.

Meanwhile, Matt could not wait to get to Rome. He sat with his parents aboard Flight 247. He'd brought his leather case full of "Lizzie evidence" and was in the process of shuffling through it, using a calculator to estimate the vast sums of wealth he'd have after he had totally ruined his sister's life.

"What've you got there, little man?" Mr. McGuire asked jovially.

"Uh, nothing," Matt replied.

Mr. McGuire leaned over and pulled out the Internet photo of Lizzie and Paolo. Mr. McGuire's expression turned worried. "What's this?" he asked.

"That's not Lizzie," Matt said quickly.

Mrs. McGuire snatched the photo from her husband's hand. "Yes, it is. I know my daughter. I got her that necklace."

Faster than a speeding bullet, Matt felt the full force of Parental Power aimed right at him. "All right," said Mr. McGuire gravely, "tell me what you know that I don't."

"Dad," Matt said, "it's only a fourteen-hour flight."

CHAPTER 10

That day, Paolo took Lizzie to a rented rehearsal hall where he was going to teach her how to move and groove like a pop star.

She stepped out onto the empty stage. "This is so cool!"

"It will be more like *this* at the Colosseum," said Paolo. Sergei turned on the lights, and the theater lit up like a Christmas tree.

"*Eep!*" said Lizzie, completely overwhelmed.

"There is no time for the *eep*," Paolo told

her sternly. "You must take the stage. And if we want to convince the world that you are Isabella, you must dance—*and* sing." He popped a Paolo and Isabella CD into a boom box and pressed PLAY.

Paolo began lip-synching, then turned to Lizzie. "Just move your mouth along with the words," he said.

"You want me to lip-synch?" she asked.

"Yes. Just like Isabella," Paolo replied.

Lizzie gave it a try, but she was definitely no Italian pop star. Paolo gave her a look and turned off the music.

"Was I awful?" she asked, feeling mortified.

"Yes," Paolo said. "But it helps to sing."

Lizzie was surprised. She thought lip-synching was just that—moving your lips and nothing else. "Really sing?" Lizzie asked, just to be sure.

"*Sì*. It makes it look more real."

"But—you weren't singing," she said.

"Of course not," Paolo replied. "I'm not warmed up. And anyway, I must save my voice for the performance."

Lizzie looked unsure. Seeing her expression, Paolo added, "Lizzie, no one will hear you. When you're up onstage, your microphone will be turned off. You must try. Please."

Lizzie tried again, letting herself sing out loud. She actually sounded pretty good. Paolo looked surprised.

"Brava!" he cried.

Hey, now you're a rock star!

"And now we dance," said Paolo. "You must rehearse with these." He held out a pair of shoes.

Lizzie's heart sank. Stiletto heels! "Will there be a curtain surrounding the stage?" she asked.

"No," Paolo answered, giving her a curious look.

She refused to explain. All she said was "Good."

The rest of the day was spent dancing with Paolo. On the one hand, it was wonderful. He was cute, graceful, cute, helpful, cute, and . . . cute. Lizzie felt totally awkward, but she honestly thought she got better as time went on. Practice wasn't quite making perfect, but she was improving. Soon even the stiletto heels started to feel kind of manageable.

it's true—divas have all the fun.

By the time Lizzie got back to the Hotel Cambini that night, she felt like she really might be Isabella. It was weird to feel so close to somebody she'd never actually met. She crept into her room, bursting with excitement, and found Kate awake. "Hi. Oh, good, you're up," Lizzie said excitedly. "I had the most unbelievable night, and I have to go get Gordo, and I'll tell you both."

"You won't find him," Kate said.

Lizzie didn't like the serious tone in Kate's voice. "What? Where is he?" Lizzie asked worriedly.

"Probably getting on a plane right now."

Lizzie felt a dark cloud gather over her bright, sunny world. "Huh?"

"He totally covered for you," Kate said, "and got himself kicked off the trip."

The cloud released a storm of emotions in Lizzie: sorrow, gratitude, but mostly, guilt.

"He what?" she cried. "No way . . . I mean, why would he do that?"

Kate looked at Lizzie incredulously, as if she were wearing shoes that didn't match her outfit. "You're seriously asking that question?"

Lizzie ran down to the lobby. "Giorgio!" she cried. "You've got to call the airport quick, and find out if Gordo's plane has left yet!"

Kate got off the elevator.

"I can't believe Gordo would do that for me," Lizzie said to her. "Giorgio's calling the airport. Maybe he's not on the plane yet. I could go to the airport and . . ."

"And what?" Kate asked.

"I don't know," said Lizzie. She had no idea what to do. And no best friend to go to for advice.

At Fiumicino Airport, Gordo waited to board Flight 1512, his plane back home. He felt absolutely awful. And yet, at the same time, one thought made him feel very happy: Lizzie's adventure could go on. He had done that for her. At that moment, he couldn't think of one thing he wouldn't do for Lizzie McGuire. The thought stunned him. What did it mean? Did he even want to go there . . . ?

A commotion at the other end of the terminal interrupted his thoughts, and Gordo turned, more out of reflex than real curiosity. What he saw shocked him.

Meanwhile, Giorgio was on the phone with the airline. "The plane is gone," he told Lizzie and Kate. Lizzie ran out of the lobby and into the courtyard. She sat down and began to cry.

Back at the airport, Gordo couldn't believe his good fortune. He had just spotted—Isabella! But he was having no luck getting through the wall of record company executives, personal assistants, and bodyguards surrounding the pop star. Finally, he crawled on his hands and knees through everyone's legs.

"Excuse me, Isabella," he said.

Isabella ignored him. She was busy staring at the cover of a tabloid magazine. "Who is this girl?" she asked. "I was relaxing on an island, trying to forget about this whole situation, and then I see this. Who here can tell me what is going on?"

"I can," said Gordo, from the floor. Two security women grabbed his legs and began dragging him away.

"That's my best friend Lizzie McGuire!" Gordo cried.

"Let the man on the floor through," Isabella said.

Gordo stood. "I'll have you know I didn't start out on the floor," he said, trying to restore his dignity. But when he looked directly at Isabella, he couldn't talk for a moment. She *did* look exactly like Lizzie. It was uncanny!

"I demand for you to tell me everything about this 'Lizzie McGuire,'" said Isabella.

"Well, I demand you tell me everything about this Paolo Valisari," Gordo retorted.

"I left him and all my thoughts about him on the island," Isabella replied.

Gordo sighed. "Good for you," he said. "You left him on the island, but my friend is out there pretending to be you, so you don't get sued."

Isabella turned to Gordo, confused. "We need to talk in private," she said.

"Gordo's life is ruined," Lizzie said the next morning, lying in bed. She felt the sting of tears in her eyes. "Because of me. Selfish me."

She made a decision then and there. "I'm going to turn myself in to Miss Ungermeyer." She threw off the covers and marched to the door. Kate jumped up and blocked her way.

"Listen, you'll be sent home and won't be able to help Paolo," Kate pointed out.

Lizzie felt as if she were being torn in half. Help Gordo? Help Paolo? What should she do? "But I'll never be able to get through it the way I feel now," she said miserably.

"Okay, fine, quit," Kate snapped. "But then everything Gordo did will be for nothing."

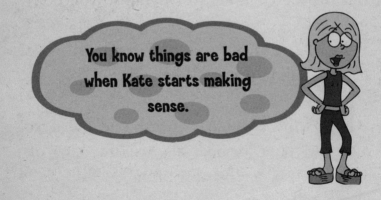

You know things are bad when Kate starts making sense.

Lizzie turned and walked back to her bed. "Well, one thing's for sure," she said.

"What?" Kate asked.

Lizzie climbed back under the covers. "It won't be hard for me to fake being sick today." And then she pulled the covers over her head.

That evening, assistant manager Giorgio was trying to deal with two very frustrated patrons. "That's *McGuire, Lizzie McGuire,*" Lizzie's mother told him for the nineteenth time.

"Yes," said Giorgio helpfully, "we are in the travel guides."

"No, no," said Mrs. McGuire, "we're the parents of *Lizzie*!"

"Ah!" said Giorgio, understanding now. "Via Liuzzi! I call a cab. Is very far."

Mrs. McGuire sighed, turning to her husband and Matt. "Anyone else want to get up to the plate?"

"Who's asking for McGuire?" Miss Ungermeyer said as she emerged from the elevator.

"Miss Ungermeyer!" said Mr. McGuire. "We are so glad to see you! We're Lizzie's parents. We need to see her right away."

Miss Ungermeyer didn't try to hide her disgust. "I've seen this before. Weak, pathetic, clingy parents who can't stand it if their precious offspring leave the nest for a mere two weeks. If you want your daughter to actually grow up into a functioning adult, you should—" She stopped when Lizzie's mother held up the Internet photo. Her eyes bugged out. "Come with me."

Miss Ungermeyer took them up to Lizzie and Kate's room. When she opened the door, a sleeping figure was in Lizzie's bed and there was no sign of Kate. "Sanders?" she called. "Where did you go?"

Mrs. McGuire sat on the edge of Lizzie's bed. "Sweetheart?" she asked. When she got no response, she pulled back the covers, revealing a human-sized pile of pillows and clothes.

Matt couldn't help it. "Cool!" he said.

They tried Ethan's room next. They found Ethan lying on his bed, eyes closed, listening to music on his headphones.

Miss Ungermeyer pulled the headphones right off. "Where is Lizzie?" she demanded.

Ethan didn't want to rat anyone out. "Uhh . . ." he said.

Miss Ungermeyer yanked open the window, grabbed Ethan's prized skateboard, and held it out, ready to drop. "Tell us where Lizzie is, or this deck will get some serious air."

Ethan's face went white as a sheet at the sight of his precious skateboard in peril. "It's possible that she's at the International Music

Video Awards, doubling for an Italian pop star named Isabella who's, like, totally her twin!" he blurted out. When he saw the disbelief on everyone's faces, he demanded, "Why does everybody always look at me like that?"

CHAPTER 11

Sergei stopped the limo in front of the Colosseum, where the IMVA awards ceremony was taking place. Looking out from the back seat, Lizzie could hardly believe her eyes. Throngs of fans, photographers, and TV camera crews lined either side of a long red carpet, on which countless celebrities were walking up to the Colosseum entrance.

Before Lizzie knew what was happening, Sergei got out, came around the limo, and opened the back door. Lizzie stepped out onto the red carpet. The roar of the crowd almost knocked her over. She'd heard that sound plenty of times before on television, but it never sounded like this. Even during the rowdiest football game! And this crowd was roaring for *her*. Well, *Isabella*-her. It filled her with the confidence she needed. She strode down the red carpet in her stilettos with perfect grace. The carpet seemed to stretch forever, and her eyes started to cross from all the flashbulbs, but it was marvelous all the same. That is, until she tripped. Oh, well, stilettos *were* awfully hard to walk in! She picked herself up and continued down the carpet.

Finally, they made it to the backstage area. The second they arrived, makeup artists and wardrobe assistants began to busily primp and poke at them. Paolo spoke to the stage manager and then relayed to Lizzie, "He said for you to enter from here, stage right. And I must enter from stage left, over here."

"Paolo, I don't think I can do it," Lizzie said panicking.

"Lizzie, you must," Paolo said impatiently. He took a deep breath and calmed down. "We've rehearsed. You know the steps and all the words. You will be great. I know."

"How do you know?" Lizzie asked.

"Because," replied Paolo, "because you shine like the light from the sun."

Lizzie smiled, flattered by his compliment. Then Paolo leaned over and kissed her on the cheek before he was whisked away by a stage manager.

A moment later, someone tapped Lizzie on the shoulder. She turned around to find— Gordo! "Oh my gosh!" she cried. "Gordo! What are you doing here?" She threw her arms around him.

Just then, a stage manager appeared and tried to lead Lizzie away.

"It's a long story," said Gordo.

"Well, I want to hear the whole thing," said Lizzie. "But right now I have to change into my dress for the number."

"No, you have to listen to me," Gordo said quickly. "Lizzie, Paolo is setting you up!"

"What?" Lizzie cried. "What are you talking abou—"

"Actually, he's setting *me* up," a voice interrupted.

Lizzie turned and saw—Isabella.

"Freaky, isn't it?" Gordo asked.

"Way freaky," Lizzie agreed.

"Way, way freaky," Isabella chimed in.

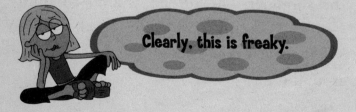

Clearly, this is freaky.

"That whole story Paolo told you about doing his own music, writing all the songs, going solo," said Gordo. "That's *Isabella's* story."

Isabella nodded. "*Sì*. Paolo is the one who synchs with the lips. Not me."

"*Isabella* is the one who wants to quit the act, and Paolo is a liar," Gordo went on. "This has all been some crazy scheme to set you up and embarrass you onstage to make it look like Isabella can't sing. He's trying to destroy her career!"

It was all too much and happening too fast. Lizzie's head was spinning. "Paolo would never do that," she said, grasping for some truth to hold on to. "I don't believe you!"

Isabella looked her straight in the eye. "Lizzie, who are you going to believe—this boy you are knowing all your life, or a boy you are just meeting who tells to you, 'You shine with the light of the sun'?"

Lizzie felt as if Isabella had punched her in the gut. True panic began to take hold. "Okay, you're here now, *you* go out there!" she told Isabella, wiping tears from her cheeks.

"But I am not blond!" Isabella said. "Paolo will know it is me, and then he will find an excuse to leave. But if we want to get back at him in front of the whole world, on live TV, we must make Paolo sing, really sing, not synch with the lips."

"But how?" Lizzie asked. "And what about me? I can't sing live!"

The stage manager walked up. "You must go now," he said in Italian, pulling Lizzie away toward the dressing room.

"Gordo! Isabella!" Lizzie cried, frantic.

"Go! Go and change your clothes, then go out there and do what you rehearsed. It will all be fine. I have a plan!" Isabella said.

Lizzie left. Gordo turned to Isabella. "So, what's the plan?" he asked.

Isabella winced. "I don't know," she said.

Isabella made her way to the soundman. "Sandro, quick, I need your help," she said. "Did Paolo bring a voice track for me tonight?"

"No, he did not," Sandro replied. "There is no track. He said you were singing live, like you always do."

Gordo and Isabella suddenly froze. The announcer was introducing Paolo and Isabella.

The next thing Lizzie knew, she was onstage. Just like she'd practiced, she walked gracefully to the center, until she met up with Paolo coming from the other side. Lizzie had no idea that her mother, father, and brother were backstage. Miss Ungermeyer had bullied her way through the security guards, and now the whole backstage area was filled with Hillridge Junior High School graduates.

It was all Lizzie could do to keep a smile on her face. She couldn't really see the audience through all the lights shining down on her, but she could feel them, *thousands* of people, all watching *her*. To say nothing of the cameras that were transmitting her image *around the world*. She was suddenly afraid she might throw up, but she thought of Gordo, and her stomach settled down again.

The music started, and Paolo began to lip-synch. Then it was Lizzie's turn to start singing—she opened her mouth and started moving her lips . . . when Isabella's voice poured out of the loudspeakers. After a moment's surprise, Lizzie began lip-synching flawlessly.

Paolo, who had just had a look of complete smugness on his face, was shocked to hear

Isabella's voice. His jaw dropped. He looked around wildly, and then he spotted Isabella singing into the headset backstage. She waved to him merrily.

Paolo gulped and continued to perform. That's when Gordo made his move, sliding the fader on Paolo's vocal track all the way down.

Paolo's real voiced croaked out over the speakers. He was bad. Very bad. The audience winced.

Just then, Isabella stepped out of the wings and onstage behind Lizzie. The audience gasped. What was going on?

Isabella sang, her voice clear and true. "Sing to me, Paolo!" she said.

The jig was up. Paolo tried valiantly, but all that came out was a screechy off-key whine.

"Impostore!" the crowd cried.

The humiliated soon-to-be-ex-pop-star glared at Isabella and Lizzie then ran off the stage.

Lizzie figured it was her turn to exit, too. But Isabella spoke to the audience. "Say *buona sera* to my American friend—Lizzie McGuire!"

The audience applauded.

"Would you like to hear her sing?" Isabella asked. Lizzie panicked as the spotlight hit her. But a quick glance into the wings at Gordo's encouraging face was enough to give her courage.

That was all she needed. Forgetting about her fall in the bathtub, forgetting about the disaster at graduation, Lizzie McGuire summoned up her own confidence, took command of her own destiny, and began to sing. Really *sing*.

Out in the audience, Matt watched his sister in absolute shock. "Whoa," he said. "Lizzie *rocks*!"

Mr. and Mrs. McGuire could only agree. Their daughter was a whole lot of surprises rolled into one.

And then there was another surprise. Isabella blew Lizzie a kiss, then exited so Lizzie could finish the song all on her own.

Lizzie panicked and was about to run offstage. Stay! Gordo gestured. Lizzie looked out at the audience. They were moving and grooving—for her! The spotlight was on Lizzie. She realized it was her moment—and she was going to seize it.

Lizzie danced and sang her heart out, working the crowd into a cheering frenzy. When she was done, she motioned for Isabella to join her onstage. They held hands and bowed.

Later that night, in the courtyard of the Hotel Cambini, a huge party was underway. Photographers, press, music industry executives, the

McGuire family, Miss Ungermeyer, and the student group were all there. And in the middle of it all—was Lizzie.

Nearby, Kate and Ethan watched her. "She got everything you're supposed to get on a trip to Europe," Kate said—"adventure, romance, total confidence. You know what happened to me?"

"What?" Ethan asked.

"I went backward," Kate answered. "I thought I had everything figured out. But if all that can happen to Lizzie McGuire, the only thing I know now is I don't know anything."

"That's not backward," Ethan said. "That's hot."

"Huh?" Kate looked confused.

Ethan nodded knowingly. "Chicks who think they know everything are a turnoff."

Kate looked at Ethan, almost as if she were

seeing him for the first time. "You think so?" she said.

As if by reflex, Ethan reached out and snagged two heaping plates of spaghetti from a passing waiter, placing one in front of him and one in front of Kate. "Totally," he replied. "And what was that about not ratting out Lizzie?" He paused. "That was so—hot of you."

They smiled at each other and dug into their spaghetti. *Deliziosi!*

Gordo stood alone in the courtyard, watching Lizzie smile and pose for the cameras. Suddenly, Miss Ungermeyer was at his side, offering him a sandwich from a platter.

"Lying," said Miss Ungermeyer, "even for a good cause, is beneath you, Mr. Gordon."

Gordo took a sandwich and got right to the point. "Am I on or off the trip?" he asked.

Miss Ungermeyer gestured toward Lizzie.

"Miss Diva explained the whole thing. In the Ungermeyer universe, helping out a friend erases brownnosing. Make sure you put this trip on your college application."

She smiled and clinked her glass against Gordo's. He smiled back—excellent! Things were looking up!

Giorgio sat next to Matt near the fountain.

"I bet you're wondering who is Lizzie?" Matt asked the hotel manager. "Where did she come from? What are her most embarrassing moments? I can offer you access to all of that at very competitive rates." He flipped open the screen on his video camera and showed Giorgio the tape of Lizzie singing in the bathroom.

"When in Rome," said Giorgio.

"Yeah! Yeah!" Matt said excitedly. "We do as the Romans do."

Giorgio pulled the tape out of the camera. "No," he replied, "we do not blackmail our sisters. As a former commander in the Italian navy, I am ordering you to leave the country." He stood up and tossed the tape into the fountain. It landed with a splash.

"Hey!" Matt cried.

Gordo had enjoyed about enough of the evening's festivities. He was all mingled out. He left the courtyard and headed toward the elevator. He pressed the UP button.

"One sneak away for old times' sake?" a voice asked. It was Lizzie. They smiled at each other and jumped into the elevator.

On the rooftop of the Hotel Cambini, Lizzie and Gordo looked out at the twinkling lights of Rome.

Lizzie felt exhausted, but completely satisfied. What a night! Paolo had been exposed to the world, and Isabella's career was now secure. Lizzie's mom and dad had praised her, though they were still grounding her for the rest of the summer. Matt had told her she was cool—no small compliment from him. Her classmates, including Kate, had congratulated her. Miss Ungermeyer hadn't yelled at her. Yet. Everything was right with the world.

"Are you going to miss it here?" Gordo asked her.

"Kate says I should just stay and have my stuff shipped over from home, because it'll never be the same when I leave here," Lizzie answered.

Gordo snorted. "Well, she's wrong, as usual. You didn't need to be in Rome for all this to happen."

Lizzie looked unsure. "You think?"

"Trust me," Gordo said. "You had it in you all the time."

Lizzie looked at Gordo. He was her best friend. He had always been her best friend. And he'd made it clear that he'd do anything for her. What if . . . what if he were *more* than just a friend. . . ? "Gordo," she said slowly.

"What?" Gordo asked.

Summoning up her confidence, Lizzie leaned over and gave him a kiss. Not on the hand. Not on the forehead. On the lips.

Gordo gulped. "Um . . . thanks . . ."

Lizzie smiled. "You're welcome."

They stared awkwardly at each other for a moment. Then Gordo said, "So, should we go back to the party before we get in trouble?"

Lizzie nodded. "Yeah. I can't afford to get into any more trouble."

A few days later, Miss Ungermeyer and crew were winging their way back home. Lizzie and Gordo sat side by side, asleep.

Lizzie stirred, and woke to find herself face-to-face with Gordo. She smiled. Things were back to normal, but everything was different now.

Smiling, Lizzie settled back in her seat, closed her eyes, and began to dream.